For Emilie, Liam, and Faye.
—BH

For my little dog Algy, he's not a bunny but he is funny.
—SJ

ZONDERKIDZ

I Love You, Funny Bunny
Copyright © 2019 by Zondervan
Illustrations © 2019 by Zondervan
Written by Barbara Herndon

Requests for information should be addressed to:
Zonderkidz, 3900 Sparks Drive, Grand Rapids, Michigan 49546

ISBN 978-0-310-76541-7

Interior design: Ron Huizinga

Printed in China

18 19 20 21 22 /DSC/ 21 20 19 18 17 16 15 14 13 12 11 10 9 8 7 6 5 4 3 2 1

I Love You, Funny Bunny

I love you, Funny Bunny,
from your whiskers to your toes.

I love the way you hop around

and wiggle your cute nose.

I love the way
you make me laugh,

then melt me with
your smile.

And no one in this great big world
can match your sense of style.

I love it, Funny Bunny,

when you sing your favorite song.

I love it when you stop and ask
if I will sing along.

I love your sense of wonder,
  when you first see something new.

I love the times we cuddle close
and share a book or two.

I love to hear you call my name
in your own special way.

Mom

I love it when you hold my hand
and talk about your day.

I love your generosity,
your gestures from the heart.

I love you, Funny Bunny.

You're my favorite work of art.